On my very first school day I met...

By Norman Stiles • Illustrated by Bill Mayer

MILK & COOKIES PRESS ™

For Ellen, my family, my friends,
my in-laws, and my fellow outlaws.
–NS

For my climbing buddy, Forest.
–BM

A publication of
Milk and Cookies Press, a division of ibooks, inc.

This book is a work of fiction.
Any resemblance to actual events or locales or persons, living or dead, is entirely coincidental.

ibooks, inc.
24 West 25th Street, 11th floor, New York, NY 10010

The ibooks, inc. World Wide Web Site address is:
http://www.ibooks.net

ISBN: 0-689-03924-7
First ibooks, inc. printing: July 2005
10 9 8 7 6 5 4 3 2

Editor – Dinah Dunn

Associate editor – Janine Rosado

Designed by Edie Weinberg

Library of Congress Cataloging-in-Publication Data available

Manufactured in China

On my very first school day ever I met friends more fantastic than I had met yet.

A dragon with three heads, all the same size
with his three dragon tongues and his six dragon eyes
with a cute little face on his tummy so round
who giggled and asked where his mom could be found.

And...

A dragon with three heads, all the same size
with her three dragon tongues and her six dragon eyes,
but *no* cute little face on *her* tummy so round.
She was his mom! I'm not fooling around!

And...

Three birds in a box, who knew how to fly it.

And...

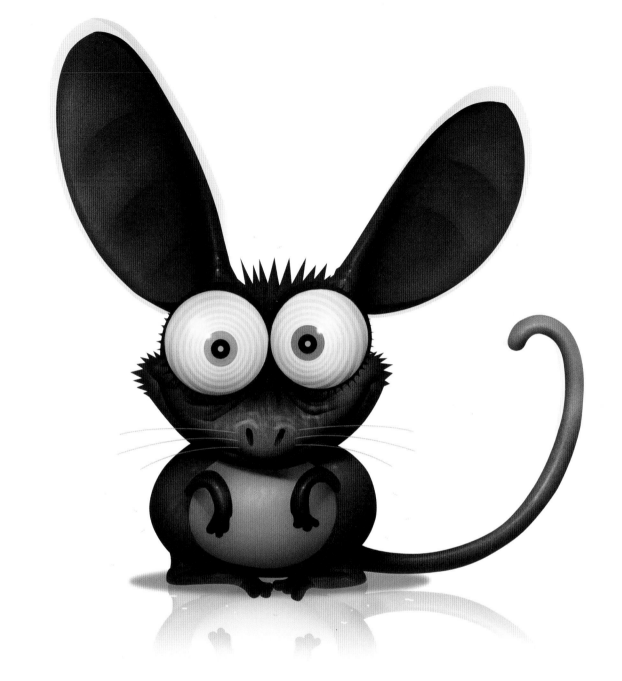

A mouse with big ears, who really liked quiet.

And...

A girl with a pull toy, who
came with her brother,
who showed me a drawing
they did of their mother.

And...

A sweet dinosaur
who was big as a bus
Who said: "Hi, howdy, ho!
I'm a Smile-o-saurus.

I'm happy, so happy, so happy we met.
Meet my horse-cow-flamingo-pig-froggy-duck pet!"
And...

A bike riding dino who rode really fast…

…who surprised a penguin who screamed when he passed.

And…

A poor blue gnu who was feeling quite sick.

And...

A yellow-eyed clock who said "Tock, tick, tick, tick!"

And...

An ape who stood up on five toes for a while,
with his tongue sticking out from the side of his smile.

And...

The silliest monster that I've ever seen!

And...

A chameleon who said,
"Look, I'm blue…

…now I'm green!"

And…

A brother whose sister bounced high in the air.

And...

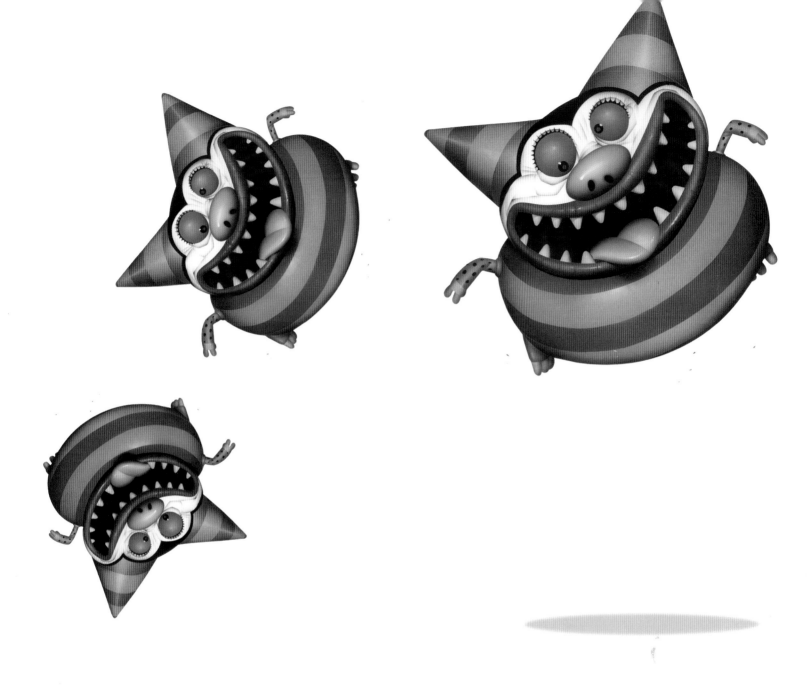

That is not all. No, I'm not finished yet.
On my very first school day ever I met…

A cow who spilled paint, yes paint, everywhere! **And...**

A teacher whose lips were
bright ruby red,
with a camera that grew
right out of her head!

And... And...

On that very first school day ever **they** met

A friend more fantastic than **_they_** had met yet. . . .

Me!